When Grandpa "Rares Back"

By
Evangeline Nicholas

Illustrated By
Angelo

My grandpa is tall and lean. He reminds me of a big, tall tree swaying back and forth in the wind. He can lean way back on his legs.

He knows many, many things. He's like a big walking storybook. And when he stands up to tell you something serious, he always "rares back" on his double-jointed legs.

Grandpa loves me and I love him. On weekends, we go to different places together.

We have a lot of fun going here and there. We go to the movies, or the zoo, or just walk around the neighborhood. I especially like it when Grandpa takes me to the playground.

Grandpa always gives me good advice. Some of his serious sayings are, "You should mind your momma," "Friends are for keeps,"and "First impressions are very important."

You can learn a lot listening to adults tell stories. That's why I stop right where I am to listen to Grandpa!

8

Grandpa told me that he used to help old man Rowe at his barbershop. Grandpa liked to listen to the older guys tell their stories. He said, "That's how I found out that neighbors need to help each other. The guys at the barbershop were always taking up collections to help someone."

I learned from Grandpa how he worked on the railroad to make money to care for his family. He said it was hard work, but that you can do anything if you put your mind to it.

Well, one day Grandpa's saying about putting your mind to it really helped me out. I was really worried about winning a part in the school play.

Everybody at school wanted a part. I carefully studied and practiced all the lines. My aunt even helped me learn to say each word just right.

Well, when it was my turn to try out, I wore my best outfit. I wanted to make the right impression. I just thought about Grandpa "rarin' back" on his legs and putting his mind to it.

I got up and tried to stand really tall. I pretended that I could "rare back" on my legs and thought about what Grandpa would say. I used my best voice and said those lines just so.

And guess what? I won that part in the play.

On opening night my whole family was there to see me do my best. Grandpa was so proud of me when he saw me "rarin' back" on my own legs. I sure did put my mind to it.